the
Winter
of the
Leechman

the
Winter
of the
Leechman

Mary Bazylevich

Mary Bazylevich (signature)

Thistledown Press Ltd.

Canadian Cataloguing in Publication Data

Bazylevich, Mary, 1933-

The winter of the leechman

(New leaf series)
ISBN 1-895449-52-9

I. Title. II. Series

PS8553.A98W5 1995   C813'.54   C95-920159-9
PR9199.3.B39W5 1995

Book design by A.M. Forrie
Cover art by Lia Sunshine Weingeist Harned
Set in New Baskerville
by Thistledown Press

Printed and bound in Canada
by Kromar Printing
Winnipeg, Manitoba

Thistledown Press Ltd.
633 Main Street
Saskatoon, Saskatchewan
S7H 0J8

Acknowledgements
"Water Rites" was first published in *Grain* and "Me and Mr. Beauregarde and My
Grandfather" in *Western People*.
"Coyotes" was broadcast on CBC Radio.

This book has been published with the assistance of The Canada Council
and the Saskatchewan Arts Board.

This book is dedicated to my children
Thomas Andrew
Ellen Rose
and to
Andrew Thomas, who is all of us together

Contents

The Winter of the Leechman

She cries out in her delirium. She whispers too, sometimes, frantic gasps trailing off into sighs. Her sons stayed with her till nearly midnight, bright with jokes and smiles in her presence, somber and distracted when out of her sight. The night nurse convinced them to leave.

I'm alone with my patient, waiting for morning.

Now in the quietness of the hospital night, she sleeps a drug-induced sleep while I read a magazine. I study her face, the bones so near the surface, and wonder what it's like, this journey into an alien dimension. I wonder if she regrets leaving the softness of her life, a softness gained with calloused hands and days which began and ended in darkness? She's told me she sometimes dreads the return of the pain between narcotic doses, but gives little sign of even this weakness.

The Crab is silent, but I know it's there, slowly burrowing into her bones. There's no rhythm in the rise and fall of her breathing.

It was early in November, with the first snowfall cleansing the night with lazy feathers, when I first heard of Kathy's Leechman.

She had been sleeping fitfully, more awake than asleep. I was watching her and the night traffic beneath her window.

"Mamma! Don't leave me." She cried out, her tongue shaping the words imperfectly. Then, on the verge of consciousness, frantically, "The Leechman, the Leechman." And I thought it was fear in her voice until later, when piece by piece over the following weeks, she brought him to me as an entire human being. Then I could see him, and understand why he'd come back. I felt as though I, as well as Kathy, haunted that time and that place where the Leechman came.

But waking that night, she had said nothing about her dream, and I didn't ask.

Watching her body made passive by the sedatives, giving its life to the cancer, I compare her to the others I've been with as they waited to die. They're all there today, in a way I can't really understand. Suddenly I feel cold in the cloying warmth of the tiny room.

I feel I've lost some of my own strength, letting Kathy draw me into her life, her past. I wish I had kept a greater distance between us. It isn't good, I know, letting her memories become lucent in my mind, letting the Leechman become as real to me as he is to her, letting the images of the child Katerina's destitution turn my bones to water. As though from another time and place, Kathy's voice speaks clearly: "A leechman cleanses the body of its poisons. By this cleansing, he heals."

Startled, I look to see if Kathy's awake, if she's spoken the words, but she's in a deep sleep. It was not her voice I heard.

Kathy's illness has altered the way she counts time. The years no longer have numbers. They are, to her, connected only by events. The Summer of First Communion, the Year Tim was Born, the Autumn of the Red Sky. Her conscious mind must have forgotten about the Leechman until one day when she spoke of the local merchant giving her a free box of wax crayons.

"He was a wonderful man. A Jew. Always asked if I got good marks in school." Eyes bright with the memory of the unexpected gift, she had smiled. Then the smile melted away as her eyes became wide, looking past me into her own private distance. Finally she spoke the words which began the return of that January. "I remember! I remember when it was! It was the Winter of the Leechman! It was the year before the war."

She began to tell me a little about him then, as the synapses sent the pieces of the time from one to another, each bit of remembering stimulating another. But something about that winter was so private that she often stopped her telling about it, withdrew into a reverie I could not presume to interrupt.

One day, after one of these quiet introspections marked by little smiles and, more often, by a certain sadness in her eyes, she asked, "Have you ever lost someone you'd have given your life to save?" And I said "No."

She had looked at me and nodded, her eyes accepting this emotional weakness in my character.

I stand at the frost-trimmed window. Across the street large houses squat in deep cushions of snow. They reflect the yellow light of street lamps, outline the starkness of maple limbs, emphasize the shapes of junipers crouching against the walls. They have magic, these houses. Networks of hidden pipes and wires form webs to protect the people in them from the spirits of cold and darkness. But what I really see is Kathy's house coming to me across the decades.

Kathy's house had no magical shield.

The year is 1938.

It's a January morning, six o'clock, the sun three hours away. New snow has come during the night. It covers the older drifts, sparkling with the sharpness of frozen diamonds under a full moon. Bush-rabbits hop among the buffalo-brush clumps, visible only as duller patches of white moving across the spangled whiteness, leaving shadowy trails in their wake. They are eating the tips of the bushes.

In this sea of shadowed whiteness Kathy's house huddles low, as though trying to burrow deeper into the surrounding drifts. Its shed roof is a dark line above the frost-coated windows. Unlike most of the village houses, this one has not yet had the chinks between the logs filled with clay plaster, or been covered with wooden siding. It was built too recently.

Inside, the plaster has been hastily applied. The rough surface, however, is meticulously whitewashed. There are hand-woven lengths of heavy cotton, wool blankets, and lap rugs hung on the walls for insulation. Some of these hangings have frozen to the whitewash.

Kathy has been sleeping in the double bed between her father and mother. She's awake now, wishing she could be in her own small cot, away from the sound of her father's snoring. But it's too cold for her to sleep alone — even *she* knows that.

She thinks of summer grass springing sharp under her bare feet, of berries on trees, sun on her arms. Dreams a fantasy of catching a bird in her hands — maybe one of the tiny black and white ones, of holding its lightness for a time, of flying with it to the Old Country, where there is no winter.

I draw away from this dream which seems too real to be a dream. My own time and place are enough for me. Soon the people on the day shift will arrive, a flurry of scrubbed bodies and clean uniforms. There will be thunder in the hallways as carts with food, fresh linens, and nursing supplies are wheeled into position. Nurses and aides, perky as sparrows, will dart whitely from room to room, their numbers multiplied with the arrival of morning.

Waiting for Kathy to wake, I think of the night things changed between me and my patient. She had been restless, and we had walked the corridor like midnight ghosts, with only the shuffle of Kathy's hospital slippers revealing our presence, and the occasional *ping* as the valves on her i.v. apparatus bounced against the pole.

Afterward, she sat on the edge of her bed, catching her breath. Her pulse, as I supported her taped wrist, was erratic.

"I'm going to die." The words lingering in the little room with nowhere to go, nowhere to lose themselves.

And I answering the only possible, the unforgivable answer: "Yes."

After that, a new feeling between us. Trust. Our secret, the fact of Kathy's certain knowledge shared with another.

In the following days, she wrote letters during the more sleepless nights, one for each of her loves, as though finally, and only now, she was prepared to open her hands and let them go.

Her sleep this night is deep. Suddenly, she stirs, and I see the glisten of sweat on her arms, where the light from the corridor strikes.

The med-nurse comes in once, rustling like wind-blown paper. She leaves capsules. "Let me know if she wakes."

"Yes. I'll let you know, Mrs. Boyd."

Moments later, Kathy stirs, her eyelids flutter. I go to the door and find Mrs. Boyd, still making her rounds with the med-chart.

There's a startling clarity in Kathy's eyes, the feverish glaze gone. She smiles at Mrs. Boyd. "I feel so damp. I need to get up."

"You can get up after we clean you up a bit." She smiles the bright Head-Nurse smile which never seems to reach her eyes. "But not for too long. Maybe you can sit in the chair until breakfast." She leaves Kathy's medications on the overbed table.

Kathy looks like a pallid gamin, the years somehow stripped from her face, her short hair standing in damp peaks, gown clinging damply to her bony shoulders. The air is foul with the stench of sweat and urine, medicines and antiseptic. "Oh God. I'm so hungry."

"Breakfast will be here in a couple of hours. I'll get the girls to find you some yogurt for now."

"I suppose you think I'm pretty fussy for a dying old woman."

"Yeah. Sure." And I proceed to give her a sponge bath. She's so thin, sitting in the huge armchair while I change her bedding.

Her smile is happy, as though this dark morning is a jubilant occasion.

The shift changes just as I've finished the accordion fold in her spare blanket. "I feel so good," she says. "Like I haven't even been sick." She smiles, but behind the smile is a stillness I've learned to dread.

It's still dark when I leave the parking lot, if the city can ever be truly dark, even during the long nights of January. The new snow is not yet spoiled by the morning-rush traffic. It sparkles in the wash of the headlights, a field of polished gems.

In spite of the car's warmth, I feel a chill like cold water pouring over my skin. I see Kathy's face as it was when I left her waiting in her room. Too happy, too young, too beautiful.

I stop the car in my driveway. The lawn beside it is a spangled oblong, but when I scoop up a handful of the sequined whiteness, the magic in it disappears. There are no diamonds. It's just snow, frozen water.

My house is warm when I come into the kitchen through the garage-side entrance. Winter never seems to enter this place — the window ledges crowded with blooming plants, the walls lined with shelves of books. Here, it's possible to shut out the world beyond the lace-curtained windows and live a life of one's own choosing. Except on days like this day.

Today I need to distract my mind, to cleanse it of its premonitions. I make a self-indulgent breakfast of cheese omelet and melon, rye toast and green tea, taking a long time to prepare it. Before it's made, I've already lost my appetite. I feed most of the omelet to the cat, the melon to the budgies.

Drowsiness finally comes just before noon. I feel tired and empty inside, as though I'd been weeping for a long time. The bed is a puffy cocoon around me. The room, dim behind blue shades, is a secluded cave and I a troglodyte hidden away, hibernating. I give my thoughts to the softness of sleep.

* * *

The house in front of which I stand is the same house I've been to before. It's still winter here, as though in this place it will never be anything else. Kathy must be here, for I hear her voice bidding me 'Enter' and suddenly I'm inside the frozen house, little more than a hut with a shed built against the side of it for the cow and a few chickens.

I'm aware this is a dream, a lucid dream whose progress and outcome I'm capable of influencing with my own will. Still, I'm not familiar with surroundings such as these, don't know how to direct events in this strange dream-time. So I only wait and watch, making myself small and dark in a corner of the room.

Kathy sits on a low stool in this room, dressed in a heavy wool sweater over a long-sleeved undershirt. Her wool trousers are tucked at the bottom into laced felt boots. Braids fall from under a fitted red cap tied under her chin. She's listening, fascinated, to the crackling sound the cast iron wood-stove makes as it begins to heat with the first fire of the morning.

Kathy shivers as she waits for the warmth to begin.

She watches her father as he puts on his Old Country sheep-skin coat, his fur cap he brought across the ocean. He's going to the neighbour's place to get the daily quart of milk. His own cow will freshen in a few months. In the meantime, they must buy milk.

The straw-filled mattress rustles as Kathy's mother prepares to rise from the bed. Her belly is large with the child she expects will soon be born.

The mother is small and dark, her movements quick, jerky, sometimes fumbling. Her hair is cut in the flapper bob popular in the previous decade, a plain cut contrasting sharply with her pretty doll-face. She seems not to notice the child, but dresses quickly, shivering. Breaking the ice in the water pail with the dipper, she fills the kettle.

The woman smiles and takes off the child's cap, undoes her braids and makes new ones, saying morning prayers as she works. Her husband comes in, bringing a quart of milk still warm from the cow, and a blast of icy air.

"I have to go out again." He says it regretfully, as though he'd rather not go.

"What? Where are you going? It's still dark!"

✓ "Madame Cherevyk says the Leechman is coming on the train from Winnipeg. Today. It could be anytime, maybe soon. Who knows when the bosses will decide to send a train? I want to give the station agent a message for him."

"But drink a little tea first. The water will boil soon."

"No. I must leave a message first. Who knows where he'll go? Maybe to someone on a farm. I'm not able to walk far in this God-forsaken cold."

And so he leaves and the child asks her mother, "Who is this Leechman who is coming?"

She gets only vague answers and a suggestion that she go and draw something with the new crayons the Jew gave her. "He will be disappointed," her mother says, "if you don't make something nice."

Somehow it's become afternoon, and the father waits at the window facing the village. Another train has come, but no one is coming along the path through his tiny field. Then from the opposite direction, from behind the windowless side of the house, a grating jangle of harness-bells and the harsh crunch of steel runners on hard snow as the drayman's freight sled approaches the door.

The man they welcome at the door is short and round, unlike Kathy's father. His clothes are bulky and numerous, a little shabby but all in the style of the new country. He carries a small valise. ↱

Kathy follows him with her eyes as he unwraps first himself, then the small bundles bound against his chest. Noticing her scrutiny, he brings a taffy sucker from one of his many pockets.

"This is for you." Kathy's relieved to hear him speak the language she understands.

"Thank you." She says it almost in a whisper.

"Don't be afraid of me. I've come to make your father well. So he can work."

The dream changes, as dreams do, quite suddenly. Kathy's father is lying on a long table, still and pale. The little round dark man with curly hair is warming the insides of small glass cups with a candle-flame, then setting the warmed cups onto the father's back. Kathy's frightened to see this happening. She wonders at the purpose of the cups, wonders if they hurt.

"This doesn't hurt," the stranger tells her. "It will take away his sickness."

He takes something from a little box, something she can't see because she's afraid to come closer. He puts the somethings under some of the cups, the ones where small hills of flesh have risen on her father's back. Then he talks, and talks, and sometimes her parents answer, and she listens. Then he takes off the little cups, and she sees something soft and dark, like a worm but different, and the Leechman is talking about cleaning away the bad blood.

* * *

There's a soft buzzing against my ear, like a telephone with the ringer turned down low.

It's a man selling windshields and I say something I can't remember a minute later and drop the receiver. It's too early to get up. Only 3 o'clock.

I try to go to sleep again after drinking a tall glass of hot milk. This time I intend to dream a nice dream, maybe one of those I sometimes have about flying across a summer landscape, unseen, unheard, but seeing and hearing everything. Or the one about being in some tropical place where I live in a tent-house near a mysterious city. I need something to drive Kathy from my mind. I'm tired of illness and death, of signs and symptoms and omens. Such things don't belong in this house my grandfather built so long ago.

* * *

In the conference room, the head nurse gives me an update on Kathy's condition. "She says she's feeling better. Let me know if she wants anything. We're letting her do whatever she likes from now on. Nothing else we can do."

The words terse, needing no elaboration.

When I come to her room, she's euphoric. A little colour in her cheeks. "There you are! I feel good tonight. They didn't have to give me anything for pain! What a relief!"

"Then try to sleep. It's about time you had a decent rest." But she gives a negative shake of her head.

"I'm not tired." She continues to watch the movie on her hanging TV set.

The time Kathy told me about her father, she wept a little. The Leechman didn't cure him, and who knows why he lived another five years after the leeching. Perhaps it was the will of God, Kathy said. His heart frozen, broken by old griefs, he died when Kathy was ten. Dropped between the creosoted ties he carried, one on each emaciated shoulder — a cheap machine, rented by the railway company. Her words had been bitter, the only time I heard her speak harshly.

Shutting off the TV, she turns to me. "I dreamed of my daughter this afternoon."

"Daughter? I didn't know you have a daughter."

"She died. She was 16. Meningitis. I dreamed of her."

I begin to understand Kathy's acceptance of death. My words must be casual. "What was your dream?"

"She and I were walking together, holding hands. Just like we did one late afternoon downtown when she was eight. And it was snowing." Her face is radiant. "Just like . . . just like it was then. And she was eight again. So much in love with the whole world. With all of us. With herself. And the snow was so big and soft."

This is the time, I know. She wants to tell me of her dream, but I hear the words in my mind before she speaks them — the dream of snow, the dream of a dead love greeting her with joy. The death-dream of which the elders spoke at wakes when I was a child.

She says, "I want to see my children. Especially the grand-children. Matthew and Becky. Could you tell them at the desk?" Heart missing beats, I force myself to walk slowly. I give the message to the head nurse.

"No 99 on this one," she says.

Of course, I think. Of course, there's no 99 on this one.

Her face has an ethereal glow as I settle her back against her pillow. "I'm a little tired now," she says.

Her eyes close and she seems to be sleeping. There's nothing more I can do. I take her blood pressure, feel the pulse in her wrist. Her hands, aimless butterflies with nowhere to settle, pluck at the bedspread. Her eyes are shut as I quietly turn, intending to go to the nursing station.

Before I reach the door, her voice stops me. "Tell them I need to see my children. Just one more time." She sighs, then adds, "There's not much time."

The nurse-in-charge hurries to Kathy's bedside with me, but we're almost too late. Kathy says, "Too late for the Leechman." She sits up suddenly, then falls back, her eyes ecstatic, as though seeing something of indescribable wonder.

Water Rites

"Natalia! Natalia! Have you been running again? You *know* what can happen if you run too fast. Your heart will jump out of your chest!" My mother's voice is reproachful as she unties the hemp cord holding the boiler lid tight to keep the water from sloshing out onto the hot black soil.

"Nu! It's just what I expected. Half the water is gone. You've been running again. It spilled on the road. It's not proper for a girl your age to run. You're in your thirteenth summer already! You could have broken the wagon wheels."

Another time I might have told her the truth: I wasn't running, not this time, even if my breath came in painful gasps and my limbs trembled. I wasn't running. "Mr. Sander's dog chased me," I lie. Let her think I've been running. Just blame it on the dog. That's safe; my mother hates dogs.

So she dips the water out with two-gallon pails and carries it into the pantry to pour into yet another large enamel vessel. It will stay cool a long time, for its bone-chilling coldness hasn't gone away yet, in spite of being out in the bone-melting heat for nearly half an hour. She mutters her usual complaints about decent Old Country people and the uncivilized habits of the young, no doubt encouraged by new Canadian lack of respect and ignorance of propriety. And what would King George's lovely wife, Elizabeth, named after Elizabeth of Austria, think of my deportment? She clucks like a broody hen who's forgotten where she laid her eggs.

In the cooler darker world inside the house I let the fear out and it invades my cells and the air in my bedroom and the whole world seems to tremble with me. The hammers pounding inside my chest are louder now and there seem to be so many of them, hurting me, taking the air from my lungs. The danger has dissipated in action, but the fear is raging a delayed battle inside me.

There's no one to tell about what happened. You don't tell your mother, who may cause a scene, disturb the serenity the villagers pretend exists here. The news would drift with the wind, permeate the corners of every house. People would know what you'd rather have kept a secret. "She enticed them," people would say. Even the women. Forgetting other years, they'd just adjust the straps of their embroidered white aprons with an air of 'I told you so' and 'Still waters run deep.' You could become a *fallen woman*.

So you just go into the coolness of the clay-and-wattle plastered house built in the old Galician peasant style and sit on your bed in the dimmest place there is and try not to die.

* * *

It's 1944. Nothing is right, even though an important war is happening. The young men have gone away, some across the ocean, and nobody wants to think about how some of them won't be coming back. Mrs. Cherevyk next door has to think about it. She already knows her brother Peter is dead. Peter didn't want to go, but they made him go anyway and overseas, too, because everyone has to fight for freedom. Still, you wish he didn't have to go.

You hide in whatever dim place there is when something awful happens. Sometimes you hid inside your own mind. Like you did when Peter died on a beach somewhere, like when today happened. You pretend. If disturbed by anyone while hiding, you pretend to be reading, which your mother thinks is the same as studying. You pretend to be praying, which is virtuous and makes you look peaceful.

But inside, you remember it over and over. How something almost happened to you, something you've heard men in front of the pool hall talk about in vague snickering half-sentences which left you with a taste of decay. You think maybe the real part of you is gone and might never return. Maybe this is all you'll ever be again, this thing whose heart pounds in disorder while you watch all around you, watch for the next time. The danger is out of sight for now, but your body is a live wire quivering with a force you don't know how to neutralize.

* * *

It's a July afternoon when the earth is drying beneath a sea of air pressing hot against the land, shimmering, as I pull the little wagon along the dusty back road. Horse-drawn wagons use this road mostly, and people going on foot. Sometimes a model-T Ford chugs by, the English sheep farmers going to the bank in a bigger town. There are rumours they carry revolvers to protect their money, and take a different road each time to fool the rest of us who are Ukrainians, who might rob them because we're too lazy to work. They've never been robbed yet. Maybe Ukrainians are too lazy to kill for money. I don't know.

But there's nothing on the road today, not even the usual garter snakes making zig-zags in the dust. To the south of the road are two cemeteries side by side and a few large plots of land, each two acres or more, where people live a little removed from the main part of the village.

From this road which is a little higher than the streets of the village, I can see whatever happens there. On a little rise is the Catholic Hall. Once a week a man comes from another town to show movies in the hall, with a P.A. system from which he broadcasts wartime songs, a sort of announcement he's arrived. On movie evenings, I sit on the verge of the road, my bare legs green from the rain-fat grass and clover growing there lush as though there'd never been a drought. I listen to the tinny music which never changes from week to week, and always, without fail, there's Vera Lynn singing "White Cliffs of Dover" from the loudspeaker in the back of the movie-man's pickup truck, her voice a cry for the dead.

On this day there's little to show the village is alive, no movement; it's a painting overlaid with a silvery shimmer of heat waves. A faint chugging starts up somewhere near the main street. It sounds like a stationary engine, the heat waves muffling the sound of its noisy heart.

I step carefully in the dust fine as black face-powder, trying to keep my only pair of shoes clean. But the dust rises in tiny puffs as I walk against the heat. Another sound, humming louder with every second, then becoming a thunking rattle. A farm truck, faded red, shudders lazily along the gravel highway parallel to the line-road but a few hundred yards away. It slides into the distance, pushed along by the cloud of beige dust it has raised, until it and the dust are lost behind trees where the highway and the back road merge into a 'Y'.

The town well is a half-mile up the highway from this fork. I've been going down this road since I was ten, bringing drinking water and cooking water from the tested well. I do this every few days all summer. The road seems short usually, but today the heat makes it endless. Even with a wide-brimmed straw hat shading my head and shoulders, the sun is painful against my body.

The well is in the town pasture where the villagers keep their milk cows from spring until fall. There's a gravel pit near the well. My father sometimes gets a little gravel here for the chickens. Coming near the pasture gate, I see a team of horses in the shallow pit, only their heads visible. I've heard the town council

is making cement sidewalks on the main streets to replace the
raised wooden boardwalks. I'm sorry the boardwalks will be gone
for now there'll be nowhere to sit along the street and watch the
farmers coming in to shop late Saturday evenings. The men in
the pit must be hauling gravel to make the cement walks.

Carefully, trying not to be seen, I peek over the edge of the
pit. Two boys from my school are shovelling gravel into a wagon-
box. One is a kid they call Joe Louis at school. His real name is
Frederick. But he's called Joe Louis, or just Louis, because of his
fierce two-fisted assaults on *anything* smaller than himself. The
bigger boys tolerate him as one tolerates an unpleasant but
non-fatal disease. He doesn't bother the big kids. The girls call
him Fat Fred behind his back, but the drayman's daughter, whose
father is darn near the biggest man on earth, says it all the time
and Fat Fred just turns purple each time and doesn't say a word.

The other boy is Paul Durnay. Paul displays his genitals in the
classroom when the teacher's out or busy at the blackboard. He
unbuttons his fly under his desk, whispering 'Look, Jeannie,' or
'See this, Olga?' Nobody looks anymore; everyone knows what
'look at this' means when Paul says it. You'd think he'd catch on
and quit, but he still does it.

I wish they weren't there, that it could be someone else in the
pit, loading gravel. I think about turning around and going back
home very, very quietly, staying on the smooth grassy ground until
I'm back on the highway, but I don't dare come home without
water. My mother would ask questions I wouldn't know how to
answer. Could I say, "There were boys at the gravel pit and I got
scared"? I can imagine her answering scornfully, "Nu, and have
you never seen a boy before?" How could I tell her about Paul
exposing himself in school, about Fat Frederick/Joe Louis
pounding me since I first started school? If I did, it would happen
more than ever, with the older kids taunting me about tattling
again. Besides the water pails in the pantry are almost empty.

The only solution is to be sneaky and clever, to do everything quietly and carefully so they won't hear me from the bottom of the pit. Maybe the noise of shovels scooping gravel, the snorts of the horses, the jangling of the harnesses would drown out the sound of the hand-pump, the splash of water. I take off the boiler lid and set it carefully on the hot surface of the ground near the well. The piece of white cotton covering the mouth of the boiler is dusty now, but I can't shake it clean. The flare of a whiter light could attract their notice.

The pump squeaks a little as I pump for a lifetime. Then at last the water gushes into the pail I've hung over the pump-hook. Maybe I can fill the boiler and be gone before they notice me.

The water lies deep, deep. The old people say this is why the water is pure in spite of being in a pasture. The gravel, they say, strains out all the dirty stuff. All I know, the water is crystal and too cold to drink as it comes out of the spout. The boiler is half-full when I notice the silence.

There's no sound of shovels scraping gravel, no snorts from the horses. I stand very still. Then I hear pebbles rolling down the sides of the pit, the crunch of boots against gravel, a sound louder than the sudden roaring in my ears. A chuckle from below the top edges of the pit.

Before I can think what to do, they're standing on the level ground, looking at me in a way I don't like, whispering together only fifty feet from where I hesitate, trying to remember what to do, trying to remember what I did other times when I was alone and a boy was not.

"Nataliaaa!"

They stand quietly together a long moment, whispering, then step away from each other. They walk toward me with their bodies a little hunched over, and I think of gorillas I once saw in a Henry Aldrich movie. Their arms are sweaty parentheses enclosing whatever statement their half-crouched bodies are making. As they come closer with incredible slowness, I see their eyes gleaming narrow like oil-filmed water you sometimes see lying in wheel-ruts.

"Nataaa-liiia! Naaa-taaaa-lia!"

The voices creep toward me slowly as the movement of a minute-hand.

You can't scream here, in this empty space where no one can hear you, where even the cows have retreated to the coolness under the willows a little way across the bog.

The fingers at the ends of the four gorilla-arms flex and extend, preparing, preparing. The boots take small steps toward you. Closer. And closer.

The books you read tell you about romance, forever-love. They don't say what you should do in times like this. You only know something must happen, that what you do may or may not decide what will happen.

Your brain feels numb. It waits for a message to come, a message it can send to your limbs which feel only the pins-and-needles of panic. At last something comes from the edge of a consciousness which can't be your own; the orders it gives you are too swift, too vicious to have come from your own self.

A weapon! A weapon! The thought flashes into your brain and your eyes are no longer frozen as they search the scorched earth within the range of your vision. It's the first time you've considered the word 'weapon.' Before this, sticks were sticks, and stones were stones. Nothing had ever been a 'weapon.' Now there is a possibility of weapons.

You look for a stick nearby, maybe within reach of your arm, even a piece of broken half-rotted board, or a small branch a cow might have dragged from one of the willow bluffs. There's always some sort of jetsam here at other times. You'll find a nice long stick and hold it tightly in a desperate hand with your arms stretched far, far out from your body as you spin on panic-propelled feet, whirling faster and faster and the force of your body spinning will translate to wide blurred circles of destruction, dark and slivery at the farthest point of your extended forces: $E = MC$ squared. You could never understand the formula but now you know it means you might live at least until your fourteenth birthday.

Or maybe a stone, even one as small as your clenched fist. You could throw it with the force of a fury stored inside you from the time you first learned about the power of evil. The forehead of Joe Louis who is really Fat Frederick stopping the flight of the stone, like the forehead of Goliath stopped the stone from the sling of David. Maybe Paul-with-the-genitals struck instead, either of them lying wounded, bloody, repentant.

It's your own fault, you'll say. *You asked for it.*

But there are no stones, only small pebbles. No sticks either. Nothing to swing with deadly fury, nothing to throw with desperate accuracy.

The pail hangs on the pump-hook, the sun reflecting on its polished steel. If only it were not half-full. If it were empty . . .

It's so simple, something inside you says, as the boots come closer. If the pail were empty, you could swing *it* round and round yourself like a speeding comet circling the sun. The metal edge would find the flesh of an approaching enemy and bite deeply. *Empty the pail!* The command allows no argument.

So you take the pail off the hook and it seems as though someone else is doing it for you. You turn back toward the boiler to pour in the water. A dry prairie voice inside you forbids you from emptying the water on the ground. But your thrifty intentions are lost when you see the danger only six feet away now, only six feet away and moving oh so slowly with exquisite control and all the human look about it gone. Your arms jerk then with a movement your brain did not order.

The bare chests have little wiggly lines where sweat has trickled down the gravel-dusted skin. Particles of sand and food fill the spaces between their teeth. The teeth. Grinning, grinning, but not really at you.

Afterwards, you don't remember for a while how your arms moved in a frightened spasm and how the water arced out with an immensely slow beauty. It's a dream, you think, as you watch from somewhere outside yourself. The way the water moves so slowly, so majestically. A graceful plume of liquid, clear as you imagine a diamond must be, its edges rippled with crystal drops breaking away, falling, falling. The coldness of it so pure, blue as the blue in rainbows born in the hot air around the arc of water as it reaches for its target. The blood in your body has stopped with the slowing of everything around you, and there's time for you to marvel at the wonder of rainbows which come of themselves when you least expect them.

Then your heart starts to beat again and your blood tries to burst its vessels. Everything becomes faster and you see the curve of water has landed. Paul-with-the-genitals stands in an attitude of shock. The water has struck just above his open belt buckle and gushed down behind the front of his unbuttoned fly, into his boots.

I close my eyes. If they kill me for this I intend to die bravely, perhaps like Joan of Arc, with my soul intact.

Gravel stutters under hard boots and I open my eyes, ready to scream and scream and bite and kick, though no one will hear me, though they might not feel the bites through impervious layers of their need, the need to demean.

Joe Louis is running back down the gravel slope and I'm startled for a moment. Maybe, I think, maybe he's gone to get a weapon deadlier than his fists. A shovel maybe. But he calls out to Paul, "Come on! We're *already* late."

I take a chance and look at Paul. He stands in the pool of water which has taken with it some of the dusty sweat from his skin. He's covered in goose-pimples, wide-eyed, staring first at me, then at the water trickling down his body, oozing from his pants and boots, sinking into the hot gravel.

It's a look I've never seen before, and I'm not sure what it means. It may have something to do with water and how the earth can die without it. He backs away from me as slowly as he and Fat Fred had approached me, but now he's shivering. Somehow I know I won't have to scream.

My arms are too weak to finish filling the copper boiler, yet I feel guilty about its half-emptiness. This is not the frugal, decent way of doing things. My mother will ask questions but I don't care. Perhaps tomorrow I'll come back. Tomorrow when my heart has remembered its proper rhythm. Tomorrow I'll come back and get all the water I want.

Coyotes

For the first time since coming to Canada, he'll call the police. It's not a matter of courage at all. He's just as fearful of speaking — in his uncertain English — to the men in the striped trousers as he'd ever been. But now it's different; now he has a child.

He trudges through the feathery snow, fallen almost knee-deep since the previous evening. He walks with bowed head and shoulders drawn forward as though to protect himself against attack and considers how he'll tell the police about the theft.

The village is quiet, with only the sound of cows mooing and horses stamping in stables near the lanes. It's Saturday and too early for the children to be out. Nor are there any farm sleighs yet; the farmers seldom come before noon.

Mattei is a quiet man, tall and bony, inclined to growing bald. His eyes are direct, inquisitive, dark brown beneath shaggy eyebrows. He's become quieter since coming to Canada from Bukovina, afraid, always afraid, sometimes not knowing the source of his fear, but feeling the dread in his cells, familiar as the seasons. It seemed to start with the journey over the icy Atlantic, a journey unlike the many he'd made in Europe, where there were only borders to cross, linguistic and cultural borders as well as physical boundaries.

Canada, he'd been told, was different. It was vast, so vast that there was land and wealth enough to make every man a baron, a *pahn*. There were savages too, they said, but what did it matter when the wheat grew as tall as a man's shoulders and fruit trees grew wild. But still, there was a strangeness, and too much strangeness frightened him.

After living on the prairie for seven years, fears became despair, for in this part of the country, at least, there was not enough warmth to grow orchards. No body of water nearby from which to catch fish. In British Columbia, where he had gone for a few months during the worst time, riding the rails, beating the train, he had found a place very nearly like his home in Europe. There, he was sure he could make an easier, warmer life for himself, Marta and the baby. But she refused to go. Suspicious of what might exist at the end of the visible horizon. Sometimes, he felt she was perhaps a little suspicious of him. So they had stayed in this bleakness where dust filled the sky with every wind.

By the time he reaches the telephone exchange in the centre of the village the words are certain in his mind. The only trouble, he thinks, is how to translate them into English, how to speak his thoughts so the man in the RCMP station thirty miles away will understand. Well, no matter, they would surely come to investigate, and perhaps then he could fill the gaps in his sentences with hand signals.

He hardly notices the warmth inside the little building where the villagers come to make their few telephone calls. It's a liquor store too, and a bottle exchange, with a jail in the cellar meant to confine drunks and vagrants. Today there are no customers. The man who sells the liquor, connects the telephone callers, and guards the prisoners sits near the airtight tin heater watching the empty street.

"Hello, hello, Mattei. Come to buy some wine maybe?" His words are casual, but his eyes brighten with curiosity.

"I no dreenk. Everybody know this. I come to call police. You get for me."

"Police, eh? Sure, sure. Right away. What you need police for?
Somebody steal your money?" The man laughs, but cautiously,
not looking at Mattei's face.

Mattei feels the angry heat spreading from his chest, reaching
like sun rays into every pore of his body. I must not become angry
now, he thinks. Not yet. No matter what this seller of whiskey says,
no matter how he ridicules me for my poverty, I shall remain
calm.

While the liquor seller/telephone operator listens from a few
feet away, Mattei speaks to the policeman in broken fragments of
English, wondering if this complaint would mean deportation for
him and his family. You can get deported for anything, even if
you have your Canadian papers. Even if you've not done anything
wrong, even if you only report another's crime. He's accustomed
to the ways of politics, both old and new.

The heaviness in his chest eases a little when the voice on the
telephone, crackling and distant, finally says, "An officer will
come by car later. As soon as the snowplow can go out."

At least they're coming, he thinks. At least this much is
certain.

"Wait a minute, Mattei. You got to give me five cents for the
telephone." The voice stops him as he's opening the door to
leave.

He scoops coins from his pocket, hoping there are enough,
hoping the man won't see how little he has. Turning his back, he
searches among the big copper pennies hoping to find a five-cent
piece among them. It seems to him less shameful to pay with a
nickel than to pay with five coppers. He finds the coin, drops it
into the man's outstretched palm.

Outside the dilapidated building, the snow shows no signs of
human passage except for the path he'd broken walking the
quarter-mile from his small holding. Smoke rises in vertical

columns from the chimneys along the way. A sign of colder
weather coming very soon.

He knocks softly on the door of his little house. "Lock yourself
in," had been his last words to Marta before he went to telephone.

"It's me," he calls out now, falling easily into his native tongue,
no longer burdened by the need to remember English. Marta lets
him into the house.

She's very small, this wife who came with him on the ship, more
like a child. But a willful child, defying his suggestion that they
move to the west coast where, he's been told, there's a cottage on
seventeen acres of orchard, with a stream where he could catch
fish. It's like the Old Country. "I saw the place in 1936 when I
went looking for work. No one has taken it, for such places are
plentiful on Lulu Island."

She would not go to an island, nor near a mountain. She would
stay on the plains, for her sister was here, her only relative in
Canada. She defied the customs of the country too, refusing to
learn the language, wearing her Sunday apron to church, dress-
ing the traditional way.

The child is at the table at the far end of the one-room
dwelling, writing the new alphabet in wavering strokes on brown
wrapping paper. Mattei's eyes sting as he watches the boy. The
thief has stolen from the child too, perhaps mostly from the child.
He and Marta could survive on what was left, but the boy has
already been deprived of enough. He catches the five-year-old up
against him as the child runs to the door.

"Wait," he says to the questions in his wife's eyes. "Let me sit
a while. I need to think."

He sits at the bigger table near the wood-stove, stirring sugar
into his mug of tea, assessing what's left of their summer's harvest
— his wife's preserves in the bottom of the cupboards he's built.
The rain had fallen in thunderous abundance that summer and
the summer before. The cellar was full of beets and carrots,

potatoes and turnips, and mangels to give the cow at milking time. Dried beans in cloth sacks, and green and yellow peas too, sit on ledges he'd attached high up on the east wall.

The land had been kind these last few seasons. This could have been the end of the hungry times, this year when he finally had a place of his own. A cow for milk, and a few chickens to provide eggs. Strings of dried morels, boletes, and horse mushrooms hang from the ceiling, visible tokens of drought's end.

This winter they would have had meat for the child, who seemed diminished after the parched years. And his wife's womb needed nourishment for the unborn child soon to come.

The meat had been in the little wooden barrel outside the door. That was at four o'clock the previous afternoon, just before dusk. Now the barrel is empty, only the fat left at the bottom. He knows where it has gone.

His wife is weeping again, as she so often does these days, even now when some of the promises that brought them to the country are becoming real. Perhaps the pregnancy is causing her tears, he doesn't know. Perhaps he doesn't need to know. The strength is still in her, even now. She can endure much.

"Why did you listen to him? You were going to put the meat in boxes on the porch roof. To be safe from dogs and coyotes, you said. Why did you follow Saman's advice? Is your own head not good enough?"

He doesn't know how to answer.

Mattei had needed help butchering, but had no money to hire a helper. So he had bartered with Saman, time exchanged for equal time. He would help Saman cut wood with the gasoline-powered saw and Saman would help Mattei with the butchering.

It was the thief who had directed the disposition of the meat. "I'd like to alternate the fat and the lean," Mattei had said, "so whichever we want will be accessible." But Saman had said it was better to put all the fat in the bottom for now, then rearrange it in the morning.

"Let your wife decide tomorrow how she wants it. Women should direct household arrangements." It seemed sensible.

Because there were coyotes in the woods nearby, Mattei had wanted to put the meat in apple boxes which he'd stood on the flat roof of the lean-to porch. "We can put the meat in the boxes just by standing on a chair. It's not high, but high enough the coyotes won't carry it off."

But Saman said it was not necessary, easier to use the cask, then set the little table over it. "Coyotes can't move tables."

It was true. Coyotes cannot move tables, Mattei thought, and felt foolish.

Perhaps it's God's punishment. I should not have been so certain, looking too far ahead, planning everything in such a way. He mutters under his breath. *A man should never assume . . . man proposes, God disposes.* Mattei berates himself as his wife takes down the strings of mushrooms and puts them in oatmeal bags.

"We must do something." His wife's voice startles him.

"What did you say?"

"We must do something. This afternoon the church will be open for confession. It's Saturday. Do you have any money left?"

"Only a little. But how will money help us with this?"

"Money can buy a candle to light. To pray the life of the thief drips away as the wax from the candle drips away during the burning. I know you don't pray, but this time you must." Marta's words shock him.

"What? What are you saying? What if someone sees me and guesses? What if he dies then? What will happen to us? The police will deport us. They would say we committed murder by witch-craft!"

His wife scoffs, "What could anyone prove? You would be just another repentant man praying for guidance. Quite innocent."

The child has fallen asleep in the featherbed, his face pale in the November afternoon light. Mattei brings out the cache of dried herbs and a small book once owned by his aunt. The book is frayed, yellow, and Mattei turns the pages gently, muttering.

There is a way his aunt divined the truth. He lays out the yarrow stems, wishing he could remember the order. A candle. He will need a candle. And a bell. They have no bell, but perhaps a glass tumbler and silver spoon would serve as well.

"Why are you wasting time with your superstitious weeds? You already know the truth of what happened. You said the tracks were plain enough. The footprints. The marks of sled-runners. The traces of blood in the snow. What more is needed?"

"The truth. One must have truth to have justice." His voice is low and harsh, angry.

"A wise man makes his own justice. Or asks God for it."

"Maybe the police will bring our meat back. Maybe the humiliation will be punishment enough for Saman. Then I won't need to waste your God's time with my prayers."

Mattei imagines a humming in his ears. It's the sickness again, no doubt. But the humming becomes louder and louder until his head throbs with the roaring, and looking toward the road he's relieved. It's only the snowplow, spraying waves of snow along the highway, clearing the road.

"Quickly, woman! Clear these things away. The police mustn't see them. Their car is at the roadway."

He dresses in his outdoor clothes, carries in armloads of firewood from the stack against the house, glancing often toward the path, apprehensive about what he is sure will be a difficult exchange of words.

They must come in pairs, Mattei supposes, watching the officers approaching from the highway, high boots avoiding the path he broke in the morning. Yes, much better they come in pairs. The better to catch Saman and keep him from escaping. See how

carefully they observe my tracks. They'll have no trouble following the trail of the thief.

The police lift the table off the barrel, look inside. They
examine the tracks around it. One writes in a little book, asks to
see Mattei's birth certificate, his naturalization papers. Wants to
know if Mattei intends to join the army if England goes to war
against Hitler.

"I em too old," Mattei tells them. They laugh.

He shows them the trail of bootprints and sled tracks leading
toward his fence, continuing through the open gate and disap-
pearing into the white distance. He tells them Saman's name.
The one making notes writes it in his book. They walk away,
following the tracks.

Mattei and Marta wait quietly for the police to return. The
child is awake now and Marta tells him stories about how things
will be when the new baby comes from the Eaton's catalogue. The
child distracts Mattei's attention for a while, but as the sun drops
lower in the sky, he wonders why the police haven't returned. He
paces from window to window watching for the return of the
mounties.

They finally return. Mattei urges them to come inside.

"Com een, com een! You be find my meat? You breeng beck
to me?"

"Well . . . not exactly. We need evidence. Something to show
he stole your meat. We didn't find any evidence."

"What you saying? You no find meat?"

The larger one clears his throat, shifts the position of his feet.
"Well . . . yes. He had fresh meat all right. His own meat from
butchering yesterday."

"Wot? Wot you say? He no butchair yesterday. Only here he
butchair. All day. My meat! He steal et night ven I sleepink!"
Mattei's face is red, bloated with sudden anger.

"Now, now, Mr. Kalyna. Calm yourself. We have only your word against his. There's no real proof of anything."

The officer taking notes asks, "Did you *see* him stealing the meat?"

Mattei's hands are clenched now as he feels the sting of beginning tears. A man doesn't cry, he knows, not in this country. He must restrain himself. He doesn't listen to the rest.

Hopeless, it's all hopeless. A man must make his own justice here, too. But here it's not so easy, not possible to call together a group of villagers. To confront a man like Saman, to demand restitution. To threaten a man with harm, with a delegation standing firmly together as a jury. Here, everyone is a stranger, each man's life separate from his neighbour's.

The officers leave, this time following Mattei's path. He listens to the sound of their laughter in the quietness.

"They were *drunk.*"

"What?" he asks in surprise.

She repeats, "They were drunk. Didn't you notice their eyes?"

"No, of course not. I didn't notice their eyes. I was listening to what they said. Not examining their eyes."

"Must have been Saman's homebrew. Where else would they get liquor down that road? So it's just the same here. Nothing changes on the earth." She sounds disgusted. "What will you do now?"

He doesn't know what he'll do. But whatever he does he will have to do it alone. He imagines going down the back road after dark, waiting near the thief's house. Waiting for him to come out alone, perhaps drunk. Imagines holding him face down in the soft snow until he suffocates. Imagines him found too late to revive. Frozen. The police would surely think Saman had fallen while intoxicated, too drunk to stand up. His family not worried at his absence, supposing him to be occupied, maybe feeding his small herd of cows.

He rejects the idea as faulty. He might escape arrest, but surely he would go to hell for it, not immediately, but in time. At the end.

He helps Marta prepare the supper, lifting the heavier things, stooping to reach whatever she needs from the lower part of the cabinet. The thought of food repels him. But he eats, his mind wandering while Marta makes conversation with the child. He fingers the coins in his pocket, calculating the total.

Enough. Enough for what he needs to do. But should he tell Marta?

"Where are you going?" His wife and son say the words at almost the same time. He wraps a second scarf around his head. Marta looks worried, her eyes wide.

"To defend our honour as human beings. I may be late." Let her think whatever she pleases.

He leaves her gazing after him.

It's nearly dark as he trudges up the path. *So it's come to this. I'm neither a pea nor a cabbage. Nothing is truly mine. Not even my gods. Which do I choose: the old beliefs, now almost abandoned; or the new, which seem to serve only those who are already well served by their own wickedness? Which is the true God, the God we expect to keep the world in its proper order?*

Maybe it's not the God of the Jews, or the God of the Christians, nor the God the Scandinavians brought to the Old Country so long ago. Nor even the gods before them. Maybe there's no Great Plan of the Universe, no One to keep the columns in the ledgers balanced.

Nearing his destination, he regrets his abrupt words to Marta. His throat aches as he thinks of his son. It should have been better for his son. It shouldn't be this way at all. Not for his son. He wonders if Marta has guessed where he's going, what he's going to do.

There are few people at the church. The cantor in the choir
loft drones tuneless words, a ritual chant centuries old. An old
woman waits her turn to make confession.

Mattei drops five coppers in the brass money-holder near the
banks of candles before the statue of the Holy Virgin. He takes a
new candle from the box and lights it from one of the dozens
already burning in tiers of brilliance. He chooses a squat glass
holder, red as blood. The thick amber candle, pure beeswax,
drops into the cup with a soft *thunk.*

He kneels before the statue of the Virgin, the light of the
candles flickering red and blue and green and golden across his
lean face.

The entire village will know about this by Sunday afternoon.
He, Mattei Kalyna, suspected of being an atheist, even of being a
Jew, was seen at the church. Well, let them talk.

Gazing into the glow of the candles, he retreats into the
infinity of his inner self, hoping to remember a prayer suitable
for the destruction of the wicked.

Me and Mr. Beauregarde
and My Grandfather

I've always missed my grandfather, miss him even now, perhaps more than if I'd actually known him, or had at least a visual memory of him. My mother speaks of a man perpetually brown from working in the sun. I see his black hair only in my mind, bent over in his linen shirt and homespun trousers, stirring flax stems softening in a vat, or pounding them into finer strands for his daughters to spin into the strong thread he'll weave into panels on his loom.

But there's not even a photograph, nothing but the stories she tells me of his forbearance and the esteem in which he was held by the people of the district and beyond. He was not wealthy, but rich in talent, in wisdom, and in understanding. He never raised his hand against another, and his word was sacred, my mother says.

There are some things my mother brought with her across the sea to Canada. When she's gone to have tea in the village, I open the trunk and look at the shawls, the table runners, the garments he made of his own linen. We use these things sometimes, and put them away again. She won't allow them to share drawer space with the newer household linens bought in Canada. Except the tablecloth. This, she says, must be used but only to honour important visitors, or worthy workmen who come to plough the garden, or saw firewood with the gas-engine saw. It was necessary to do this, she said, as a reminder of our heritage, and of the times when she wasn't poor.

But we were not to use the tablecloth when setting out tea for Mr. Beauregarde. For him, oilcloth was good enough, she said, as I unwillingly brought out the enamel mug, and set the sugar bowl over the burnt spot in the table cover.

"It doesn't look nice, Mamma," I'd say.

"What of it? What does an Indian get at home? It's lucky I give him anything at all. I only buy from him to please my brother." Her brother's farm is next to the reserve. My uncle and Mr. Beauregarde are friends.

* * *

I'm ten years old, walking home from school, carrying my blue cardigan over my arm. September afternoon sunlight sparkles tiny gravelstones on the footpath, gilds the pale brown dryness of dormant grass and dead cornstalks. The woods burn primrose and crimson, with a few stubborn stragglers still clutching branches of summer green. This, I think, is how I want things to always be, as I skip down the slope toward our house. If my mother sees my bouncing this way she'll lecture me again. "Your heart will tear away from your chest. It happened to a girl in the Old Country. Listen to me. Walk nicely. Running is for horses."

But I don't mind if she scolds on this windless, autumn-scented day which seems like the true beginning of a new year.

As I come closer to the house I hear sounds of Mr. Beauregarde's presence — the quiet whinny of horses, the rasping whisper of strands of dried grass as the man tears it from the hayrack and forks it into a stack near the chicken-yard gate. I drop my sweater and schoolbooks on the stoop and hurry to the backyard.

Mr. Beauregarde works steadily, stacking a little way from the small cowbarn where the hens also live. At first, my father wanted the hay closer to the barn. But Mr. Beauregarde refused to stack it there. "Not a good place. Too low. Water comes here. Hay spoils," and had followed his own wisdom. No one questions him now, and my mother doesn't bother to inspect what he's doing, doesn't make suggestions in her usual language of part Ukrainian, part hand signals as she once did.

Hay dust drifts in spangled motes around the Indian as he stands tall on the rack. He acknowledges my presence with a slight tip of his dusty felt hat, then once again attends to his work, the stack growing a little higher, the rack a little emptier, with each swing of his fork. He's wearing a sweat-stained blue shirt, neatly patched at the elbows, and worn blue overalls, but there's something graceful about him, some sense of wholeness. Someday, I think, I'll learn how to do things with propriety, like Mr. Beauregarde, like my grandfather.

* * *

I'm eleven now, and have begun to worry about the Enemy coming to bomb the village. It's 1942 and Mr. Beauregarde's oldest son has been conscripted and sent to France. I weep when I'm alone, suddenly knowing what it would be like if my son was sent away to be killed, instead of Mr. Beauregarde's child. Something is happening to me, something frightening. I want to never grow up, never have sons who would be taken away for killing.

My mother still calls Mr. Beauregarde 'the Indian', even though she knows his name is Adam, a name easy enough to say in any language. It's September again and Mr. Beauregarde is unloading a ton of hay in the backyard. He's stopped to rest, sitting on an upturned applebox when I come out to look. Rolling a cigarette, he says, "Hello, Eugenia," and I'm surprised he remembers my name, or that he ever knew it. He tucks the cigarette carefully into one of his overall pockets, saying, "Never smoke by hay or straw. Burn everything." I nod, trying to appear wise. I wonder if he carries pictures of his son, the one in France. Maybe he doesn't, I decide, and I know I don't have the courage to ask anyway. I go into the house to help my mother set out Mr. Beauregarde's simple tea.

When he's gone I go to the haystack to look for moss between the layers of brome. Its laciness enchants me as it has always done. I press it carefully between the pages of an old school-text. When the winter seems too cold, too long, I'll look at it and feel assured that summer will come again at its appointed time.

* * *

The next summer I go with my cousin Tonia to pick saskatoons. She's ten years older, someone I trust and admire. We take the horse and buggy, and I wonder why we don't walk to the saskatoon bluff as usual. But she drives the horse past our favourite picking spot, across the field, tells me to open the gate at which we eventually stop. "Where are we going?" I ask.

"We're here. This is where we're going."

"Whose place is this?" I know it's not part of my uncle's farm.

"This? It's the reserve," she says brightly.

"Shouldn't we ask somebody about picking here?" There are no houses visible, only bush, but as we drive along the wagon trail and around the edge of the willowbunch, I see some houses. There are three of them, one has two storeys, and all are clay-plastered on the outside, like the houses of Ukrainian settlers.

"No," says Tonia, "we don't need to ask. They always let us come here. They told Father it's okay." And she ties the horse in a shady spot among the trees.

As we pick the dark sweet berries into the lard pails, tied around our waists to keep both hands free, something about the Indian houses nags me. Something odd, out of place.

"See?" Tonia says. "Aren't these better saskatoons?"

I marvel at the size of the berries glowing against the dull green leaves of the bushes. And as I look around my gaze rests once again on the houses. Then I realize what's wrong about them, about the surrounding meadow.

"Tonia," I say, "don't these Indians have any little children?"

"Sure they have children," she says, sounding a little surprised. "Why do you think they have no children?"

"Why don't they play outside?" I imagine that perhaps they might be shy of white strangers.

"Because they're not here. Only the babies, and right now there aren't any babies. The rest of them go to the Indian school. In Lebret." She doesn't look at me but picks faster and something about her manner says I shouldn't ask any more questions about Indian kids.

* * *

During the winter of my fourteenth year Mr. Beauregarde coaches the boys' hockey team. The war is theoretically over. I'm in high school and confused by the changes intruding on my life. Mr. Beauregarde, who's a natural phenomenon as far as I'm concerned, shouldn't be engaged in a violent thing like coaching hockey.

Everyone from the high school has been ordered to go to the town skating rink to watch hockey practice. The girls are in the skating shack, sitting on the rough wooden benches, reading movie magazines, painting their fingernails, some flirting with the boys. The boys make a big show of lacing their skates, discussing which hockey sticks are better, arguing about famous players as though they know them personally. Mr. Beauregarde comes in, says "Ready?" and leaves the shack, the boys following him, quietening down, skating in tight circles.

A few of the boys are still inside. A boy from my class, the quiet boy who wears dark-rimmed glasses speaks slowly, his eyes watching the toes of his skates. "Beauregarde's oldest boy never came back from the war. He got killed in France."

Sighs from the girls then and "I feel sorry for him."

The boys look uninterested. "I know," says one. "Who cares anyways?" says another. I begin to feel nauseous and leave the shack with its smoky wood-burning heater and its smell of fresh nail polish. I lean against the rink boards, feeling bile rising in my throat, watching Mr. Beauregarde as he walks among the skating boys, speaking quietly to one or another, sometimes blowing his whistle for attention. How can anyone, I wonder, even a boy who plays hockey, say "Who cares?" when someone dies? In the cold of that early December I walk slowly home.

* * *

One morning at the end of February an Indian boy shows up in class. He has no books, only a scribbler and a pencil. His clothes are neat and well-fitted, his hair perfectly combed. "It's Archibald Beauregarde, Adam Beauregarde's son," someone whispers. I'd never seen him before, nor for that matter, any other Indian child, nor even an Indian woman. It seems as though the Indian community is composed of only men, and only a few of them — quiet, reclusive, coming and going from the village like ephemeral beings from another world.

I would like to have the courage, the boldness, to speak to this boy with his downcast eyes, to ask him all the questions in my mind. *Why are the children in Lebret school and not in the little country school near the reserve? Why don't the older kids come to our high school? Why don't the Indian women come to the village for provisions, the same as the women from the farms? What do you think about, Archibald? When you're in Lebret, do you miss your parents, and does your mother cry when you go away from home? Why is your brother dead?*

But I've learned not to ask questions, so I spend the class staring at the back of Archibald's dark head. I notice that no one else speaks to him either, not even the teacher. A man in a new suit comes to talk to the principal during afternoon recess. They talk a long time.

At the end of the day I don't remember the lessons. That night I lie awake a long time, planning the questions I've become determined to ask Archibald the next day. I leave for school the next morning feeling brave enough to speak to him, but he isn't there. Every morning I go to school hoping he's returned, but I never see him again. Mr. Beauregarde doesn't come back to coach the hockey team.

* * *

Four months later when the wild roses are just starting to bloom, I set the kitchen table for high tea. I set three places, very properly, the way my mother learned from the English people she served during her first two years in Canada. Bread and butter, scones, jam, and plain syrup cookies — which she calls *biscuits* — but instead of the cups and saucers she insists I put out glasses, in the more civilized Old Country manner. She is being honoured by an unexpected delegation, two women who've never before come to visit.

They're dressed in proper Old Country Visiting Delegation style, each with a white *khustka* on her head (colours are not for weekdays) and an embroidered apron over a stylish afternoon dress. When I leave the house to go to the general store for a gallon of coal oil, they're muttering a prayer over the bread-and-butter. My mother hadn't told me they were coming, saying only, "If you know too much you'll age before your time. Your nose is already too long from poking it where it doesn't need to be. You must have gotten your inquisitive nature from your grandfather. Too bad."

In August a strange man with a tractor brings a load of hay. I question my mother. "Why is that man here? Why is he bringing hay? Is Mr. Beauregarde dead?"

"He's a nephew of Mrs. Krupka who was here with Mrs. Doshka in June. We decided I should stop giving profit to those not of our nationality. I shall buy no more hay from the Indian. No, he's not dead. But I only bought from him on your uncle's word. So what does it matter?" Turning away abruptly, she adds, "Your grandfather was like you. Always questioning."

The man charges my mother ten dollars for the hay, instead of eight. She always paid Mr. Beauregarde eight dollars. The man smiles and chatters and this seems wrong somehow, just as it seems wrong for him to be sitting at the table draped with my grandfather's linen peacocks and roses. He leaves in a cloud of gasoline exhaust, leaving the gate open.

I go to the stack after he's gone. It's in a different place now, near the barn where meltwater collects in a pool when spring comes. I look for moss in the stack as I've done every year, but this time there isn't any. I tear my finger on a rose branch nestled in a tangle of thistle stems. The hay has no summer scent, but instead a mouldy bread smell that makes me sneeze. I decide not to tell my mother. My father, as usual, is away working on the railroad. But I know he'll find out about the hay soon enough, and my mother even sooner.

* * *

My father shouts angry Ukrainian words I've never heard before, at whose meaning I can only guess. When he calms a little, he asks my mother: "Did you not inspect the hay when he came? Before you paid him?"

My mother blubbers into her apron. "How was I to suspect? I never needed to inspect the Indian's hay. This man's aunt would surely not have recommended him if he was a cheater. She knows we're poor."

He makes a sound of disgust. "And why did you not buy from the Indian as usual? Never once did he sell us mouldy hay full of speargrass and buckbrush. If the cow eats it what will happen?" He mutters, red-faced, threatening to tell the entire district about the swindler and his aunt, but there isn't time to do this before he leaves for work on the Sunday evening train, so he just tells everyone he happens to meet in the village. My mother is mortified. She refuses to leave our property, sends me to do all her errands in the village.

When my uncle comes for a Sunday visit, my father tells him about the hay. "Could you please ask Beauregarde to bring hay at the usual time. He must already have heard about this disgraceful thing. Maybe he'll be offended we bought from the swindler. Maybe he'll be proud and refuse." My father frowns, perplexed.

My uncle looks like he's trying not to laugh. "He'll bring the hay if he has any. Don't worry! He has concern for animals." He gives my mother a sideways look. "I suppose, dear sister, you ordered your wood from this worthy countryman of ours, too."

My mother goes into another room, pretending urgent business. I go with her and offer to make the tea for our visitor.

She glares at me, pink-faced. "Now you're gloating," she hisses. "Just like your grandfather, I see." She busily ties back the curtains, unties them again, opens and shuts the windows.

* * *

In the warmth of a September afternoon sun Mr. Beauregarde unloads a ton of hay near the chicken-yard gate. His horses know me well and want me to come to them, but I'm afraid of their size, their strength. I speak to them from a safe distance, certain Mr. Beauregarde won't think it strange, me talking to horses. They make contented sounds and breathe in soft little snorts. I go into the house to make the tea, a job which has now become almost entirely my responsibility.

But I'm too late, for my mother has already done it. I don't know whether I should cry or laugh, and something inside me is singing. Suddenly I'm not ashamed of having something of my grandfather in my nature, my dear plodding grandfather.

Mr. Beauregarde comes into the house, goes through the usual hair-combing and handwashing ritual at the kitchen washstand, behaving as usual. My mother watches him and I see a look of disappointment on her face as he sits down at the table, giving no sign of noticing anything different. His expression is inscrutable, but today Mr. Beauregarde is getting his tea in a glass, and as well as plain bread and butter, B.C. peaches cooked with sugar, and the sponge cake I made for the school party. ✓

I get a cup for my tea, a dish for peaches, and sit at the table. I've never sat with company before, except when relatives came. He speaks to me then, words he might have spoken to my mother if she had not steadfastly pretended, for twenty years, that she knew no English. His words are too soft to displace the air, they drift like summer haze in poplar woods.

"Your mother make this?" His rough fingertips delicately touch the green and brilliant blue peacock's tail.

✓ "No," I answer. "My grandfather. In the Old Country. Made cloth for people. Embroidered it, too. But my mother, she spun the flax into thread. Helped bleach the cloth." I want to tell him some of my mother's stories, too, of how it's possible to turn new brown cloth into white by wetting it with water then dragging it across the grass slowly, or by spreading it out to dry across the tops of leafy hedges. But I remember what my father sometimes says: *Empty wagons rattle,* and I don't want to be a rattly wagon, not while Mr. Beauregarde is here.

"Your grandfather is a good man."

"No. He's dead." It's not the way I meant to say it, but the hayman seems to understand. He nods his sympathy.

"Too bad. Good things get lost."

His eyes speak a little now, letting me see something of his thoughts. He looks sadly at my mother's back as she stands at the stove, putting fresh dill and shallots into a pot of chicken soup. I wonder if he's thinking of his dead, as well as of mine. ⌐

"You going someplace from here after high school?"

"I don't know." Suddenly I don't want to know whether I'll stay here or not. Either alternative frightens me.

"You should go someplace. Learn to be something. Maybe a nurse." I think this might be the time to ask him why Archibald didn't come back to the school, but I'm afraid to hear what his answer might be, or that he might not answer at all.

When he has eaten enough for politeness, he rises to leave. He holds his hand out to my mother. "Thank you, Missus."

She shakes his hand and says, "Tenk you. Tenk you. You breeng gud hay. My cow laike."

I look at her, my mouth open. She hisses at me in Ukrainian behind Mr. Beauregarde's back. "Nu, so I can say a few words in English. What of it? Is it a sin?" She tosses her head. "Don't stare. Go close the gate after him when he leaves. He's tired already."

I follow Mr. Beauregarde to his team and watch him hitch the horses to the hayrack. When he climbs onto the seat I say to him, my voice sounding strange in my ears, "I'm sorry about your boy. In France. It's not fair." He starts to say something, then abruptly turns away, urging his team ahead.

The new hay is sweet with the scent of long summer days and in it I find pieces of moss, but this time I don't bring in any for pressing between book pages. I'm old enough now to trust the seasons.

* * *

Mr. Beauregarde is dead now. I'm older now than he was when he came with his racks full of wild hay, and I wish I could tell him now how our lives would have been poorer without him. I think of him as someone sent to take the place of the grandfather I never saw, someone who taught me what my grandfather would have, had he not died of typhus before I was born. I see us brought together in some magical way, me and Mr. Beauregarde and my grandfather.

Sacraments

The voices sound angry; the long vowels, the hard consonants of Ukrainian speech emphasize the harshness.

"It's all one God, Woman. Do you think it makes a difference what church you go to ? It's not a matter for argument!"

"But all the same the Orthodox church has departed from the proper forms of worship. God doesn't recognize improper forms of worship."

From Eugenia's father's throat comes a sound like water boiling as his eyes flash grey fire. "How do you know what God recognizes or doesn't?"

Eugenia is tired of the arguments Sunday after Sunday, monotonous, predictable. She knows them by rote now, knows what each of them will say, how her mother will cover her lack of reasoning with a barrage of righteous indignation. She'll invoke the name of the Holy Virgin, begging Her to witness the sins of her husband, the heretic.

Eugenia greets the coming of Sunday morning with joy, but hurries through the early part of it, when she must, in the name of God and the Sabbath, tolerate all injustices she perceives to have been worked against her by her family. Once she leaves the house, however, she becomes a person of her own design.

In the bedroom her younger sister Oksana is trying on Eugenia's Sunday hat. Eugenia snatches it away and sets it carefully over her dark curls, pinning it in place with imitation pearl hatpins.

"You look like an old lady!" shrieks Oksana.

And from the kitchen her father calls out, "I heard you, Oksana. Must you behave like an animal, even on a Holy Day?"

Her mother comes to the bedroom, wiping her hands on her apron. "Are you already leaving? It's too early. No one will be there yet."

"That's why I'm going early. Because no one will be there. I'll read my prayer book until Mass."

Eugenia's mother, though she cultivates an aura of religious correctness, has never understood her elder daughter's constant church-going, attending every Novena, every Mass, all Vespers, even weddings of people not known to the family. Eugenia, for her part, feels uneasy about telling her mother her inner thoughts, her motives, or even her worries. She never wonders why, but only knows she can't expose her feelings.

God knows, she thinks. God knows I need to be alone sometimes with no one seeing what's inside my mind, when I want everything to be quiet, and beautiful, the way heaven is. She can't express even this simple feeling to anyone, and doesn't want to.

With a puzzled look, her mother says, "Nu, go then. But don't run." It seems to Eugenia that her mother has said the same words to her for all of the fifteen years of her life. She straightens the pleats of her plaid skirt, wishing her mother had allowed her to buy the light blue one instead.

Stepping down from the stoop, she feels the morning surround her, a benediction of white June light, of leafy fragrance. Along the path toward the village, wild roses grow tall, their branches twined through the wire fence between the property of Eugenia's parents and that of the neighbours. Her heart lurches at the sight of the newly opened blossoms, translucent pink shells gracing the day with their gentle scent. She lifts her face to the God she knows is watching her, somewhere far away in the depths of the sky hanging like a peacock dome over the village.

Her steps are light as she walks slowly, transfigured by a new feeling induced by the radiance of the day, by the anticipation of the new hours she'll spend in silent communion with herself and her angels, time unsullied by the demands of family.

The village lies before her, a widely scattered cluster of small houses and shops, each with its own sheds and barns. This morning they've taken on an enchanted quality, the whitewashed clay, the raw wooden siding somehow losing its shabbiness. They've become mysterious structures in a strange new landscape, the weather-muted colours soft against emerald trees and vivid sky.

Then it occurs that this renewal of place, this new awareness in her cells, may be a message from the all-knowing God whose presence she's felt since her earliest remembering.

A garter snake zig-zags, its rope of golden green scales defined by lines of black iridescence, moving across the warm blackness of the path, leaving a trail in the loose dust of the path. Eugenia smiles, thinking of how her mother would become hysterical at the sight of the tiny creature, her theatrical cries of despair, but only if there was someone close enough to hear. She, Eugenia, is afraid of no animal so small, so easy to frighten. The snake is, in her mind, a small part of this vibrant whole, the entire landscape of a universe without end. Everything is as it should be, as the priests and nuns say it is.

She knows she can ignore the sins of the villagers, whatever those sins may be. They all seem like good people, decent people, except for her parents, of course, and her Satan-possessed sister. These, she's leaving behind as she walks toward the church looming ahead of her, half-hidden behind the spires of Balm of Gilead poplars, its onion domes gleaming silver above the whiteness of painted clapboard. She'll sit far away from them, pretend for a time that she's an orphan, with no father who shuns the church, no mother whose religion is only an arrangement of

words, words that never direct the course of her actions. Are they
a punishment sent her by God, she wonders? A penance imposed
for sins she can't recall?

The brown Model A parked on the verge of the empty
highway announces the presence of the cantor from another
church, one who comes on ceremonial occasions since the
death of Mr. Yaworski, the local cantor. What feast day is this?
Eugenia wonders. Her mother had not mentioned a feast day,
nor had the priest announced one at the last High Mass.
Whatever it is, it will surely be an exciting occasion.

Across the street from the churchyard is Angela Duma's
house. From the open window comes a faraway rise and fall of
voices, adult voices, no doubt Angela's father and mother engaged in the kind of conversation one expects from parents. It's
not the kind of bickering she hears at home. So it is that she
remembers what's special about this Sunday's Mass. This will be
the day for reading the final bans before Angela's marriage. And
after the Mass, Angela's baby brother will be baptized.

An autumn evening the September past, and she was out
hunting the last of the ripe gooseberries. Not paying attention
to anything, she went from bush to bush, crouched low to avoid
the branches of the larger bushes growing along the roadside
ditch where berries of all kinds grew fat and lush. A sound of
voices, hushed and whispery, touched her briefly, and she
glanced up from her picking, peered toward the road just visible
between the yellowing willow leaves. Drunks maybe, drunks
always came to this almost-deserted road and left behind beer
bottles and sometimes coins fallen from their pockets. Drunks,
she knew, were dangerous, and did whatever harmful things they
could think of. She could hear herself breathing, the air rushing
into her body with a noise loud as a cyclone. Better to stay out
of sight until they left.

Against the glare of sunset she saw a silhouette of what seemed
to be two people walking. The voices came closer as she crouched
in her hiding place. Soon they were opposite her, where she could
see them clearly, away from the blinding rays. She exhaled slowly,
willing her heart to calm itself for there was no danger now, but
only the need to be silent. It was Angela and David. They might
be embarrassed to know she'd seen them, walking hand in hand,
stopping to hug, and to kiss for so long she wondered how they
could still breathe. Her legs were getting numb from being still
too long.

Seeing them, and hearing David, the quietest boy in the high
school saying, "You're my angel. My real Angel," she wondered
if anyone would call her 'Angel' when she became seventeen like
Angela. It didn't seem possible, because of her silly Old Country
name. What could you make of *Eugenia* that could possibly sound
nice, except maybe 'Genie' which wasn't too nice, since genies
weren't very good creatures to begin with, not being part of the
Church.

She had never seen anyone actually kissing before and no
wonder. The Church said it was a sin unless you were engaged,
√ and even then you could kiss only once, and only on the cheek,
and that was that until after you were married. Then, she guessed,
you didn't kiss at all. It didn't seem right but it was the law of the
church, and the church had reasons for all the rules.   ⌣

Soon they were at the crossroads, walking around the corner
toward the village, out of sight. Eugenia stood up, painfully, her
legs weak and tingly, and waited for their strength to return. She
wondered if anyone else knew about Angela and David.

It soon become evident that *everyone* knew, that she was the last
to find out. They talked about Angela and David at the school,
saying the two were in love, made various guesses about when
they might get married, or how they couldn't possibly get married
because David went to the Lutheran church. Eugenia wished ⌐

there was a way to know for sure, to be able to make up her own story about it, a true one, with no *maybes* about it.

Then one day at her uncle's house, she said to her cousins: 'Angela and David might get married.'

One cousin, the older one with the moustache, laughed. Eugenia felt her face and neck getting hot. She wished she hadn't said the words. It seemed that whenever she spoke, she said something stupid and everyone laughed.

Joe looked at her with pity. "Don't worry. Angela will never marry David."

How silly he is for an old person of twenty-five, she thought. Why wouldn't David and Angela marry if they were in love and already kissing and God only knows what else?

"Why not?" she asked Joe.

He laughed again. "Because that's not how it works."

She realized then that what her cousin said was true. "Oh, yeah. I forgot. He's Lutheran. She can't marry a Lutheran."

Joe shook his head. "Nothing to do with that. You don't know how things work, Eugenia. Someday you'll find out."

"Then why? Is it because they're too young? But other girls get married when they're seventeen, even younger. And Angela will be eighteen soon." Surprised at the boldness of her own words, Eugenia wondered if she'd become one of those bad girls the nuns talk about during the summer catechism.

Joe didn't seem to notice her venture into wickedness, but spoke to her as to a person his own age. "They can't get married because David comes from a poor family. Angela's father needs lots of money." He sat back in his chair, rocking back and forth on its hind legs.

Her aunt came into the room. "Why are you digging holes into the linoleum like that? Sit like a decent person." She bustled into the pantry, arranging the shelves with much clanking of pots and baking pans.

"I'll buy you some new linoleum, Mother. The next time I go to town." Eugenia thought he didn't look a bit sorry as he spoke to his mother, turning his head and speaking over his shoulder, raising his voice to make himself heard above the clanking of enamelled pots and roasters.

He started rocking again. "Yep. Angela's old man has a husband picked out for her. I heard him talking in the beer parlor yet a month ago." Joe's smile was sneaky, as if he knew a secret.

When Eugenia sat wide-eyed but said nothing, Joe continued his lesson in Things As They Are. "Angela's old man uses up money fast. You don't get beer for nothing. David couldn't buy him enough beer to keep him happy for even one day. Nooo . . . no poor boys for Angela. Her daddy would let her marry the Devil first, if the Devil had lots of cash."

Eugenia wondered then who else Angela could possibly marry.

She asked Joe, "Who?"

When he told her, she felt something inside her turning to stone. What he was saying *had* to be a lie. Like the lies he sometimes told just to see if she'd believe him. She usually did, but she could *not* believe this one.

She gasped in surprise. "Theodore? But he's so *old*! Why would she marry him? He isn't nice. *Nobody* likes him."

Joe smirked. "Angela's old man likes him. If Angela marries Theodore Chobot, old man Duma will be living in the Big Rock Candy Mountains till the liquor kills him."

Eugenia didn't know what that meant, and didn't want to ask. Asking wasn't nice. The nuns said so.

Eugenia looked at Joe with a worried frown. "What if Angela doesn't do what her father says? She doesn't have to. Nobody says she has to."

Joe nodded wisely, still smirking. "She has to. You bet your life she has to." He kept on rocking, digging the holes in the linoleum deeper.

It was hard to believe Joe, especially since her mother always said, without being specific, what a very bad boy Joe had always been, how disrespectful, and how he would most certainly go to hell.

* * *

What Joe said turned out to be true. Angela would be marrying Theodore after harvesting was over, before the fowl supper season started.

But it can't be for money, Angela thinks. It must be for a better reason. She must have fallen in love with Theodore without meaning to, like in the romance novels. Her father wouldn't do anything so mean, not to his own daughter. Having dismissed the idea of a heartbroken Angela standing before God's altar to marry an unloved and unloving man, she comes back to herself, to thoughts of the ritual of High Mass.

There are stories she hears, sometimes in the school when a few of the bad boys huddle near the cloakroom door, talking about things the church forbids you to question. She hurries away from their words, finds elsewhere to go and other things to do. For her, all things are decided, all things ordered, and there can only be truth and goodness in God's word, the word as taught in church.

Her mother was correct in saying, "It's not our right to question God's word, or how the priests behave. That will all become clear on the Day of Judgement at the end of time."

A sound shatters the stillness. Eugenia's heart lurches, waking her from her reverie. But it's only the church bell, its clear tones cutting the air with shards of crystal music. Her thoughts surface slowly, like bubbles in a jar of honey, rising unwillingly. She'd like to stay in her perfect world of June roses and white light, to be borne by the sound of bells, her spirit light as mist, into some new dimension of being.

The bells fall silent, but their echo lingers among the aspens, melding with the call of orioles from the dense bush. The girl enters the place she thinks of as her real home, the home where she's safe from harsh voices, from the demands of her family. This then, is the House of God, where all things are determined and beyond question, needing only a pure heart to believe. Eugenia believes.

The sexton is attending to the multitudes of candles, replacing the burnt-down ones, lighting them, clearing away the bits of beeswax from the linen cloths, straightening vases of spring flowers. The choir sings while behind the closed door of the sacristy, the priest takes confessions. Eugenia sits alone in the half-empty church, on a bench fronting the first pew. With her mind wandering, she sings with the choir, watching the people waiting in the confessional line.

Angela is the second in line, with three more people behind her. The priest comes out of the sacristy, walks down the sanctuary steps and speaks to her briefly, gesturing. As he walks back into the sacristy, with one of the penitents following, she moves to the end of the line.

Angela's wearing a dove-grey suit and a cream tricorn hat with an eye-veil. Her hair is pulled up high on her head, pinned under the little hat. Eugenia thinks how much older she looks this way, not at all like a girl still in high school. This is the way Eugenia would like to look sometime soon. She doesn't envy Angela for going to confession. It's not a pleasant thing, not like Communion, or Vespers, or Mass. She hates confession — having a strange man staring at her, asking her if she's done it with boys, if she's thought of doing it, and she feeling her face grow hot and saying "No. No. No . . . " Then making up sins to keep him from staring at her, to make him happier, and so committing a *real* sin by lying, then confessing *that* sin, the only real one. She wants only God to know her private thoughts. And maybe the angels.

Glancing cautiously over her shoulder, Eugenia looks for Theodore. He's there, in his family's pew, he and his parents, all of them looking sad and mean at the same time. Theodore's mouth is a thin lipless line, and there's no life in his eyes, none at all, not even when he looks toward Angela. Seeing Eugenia looking at him, he shakes his finger at her in disapproval.

She hates her cousin Joe a little now, and is ashamed of hating him, and wishes she could pity him for how he can't see things. How bitter life must be, she thinks, if one sees only what is painful to the spirit. Maybe if he hadn't spoken aloud about Angela marrying Theodore, it might not have happened. It's bad luck to say things like that. It can make them happen.

The sacristy door opens cautiously and old Mr. Kuzyk emerges, hobbling, his confession finished and only Angela left waiting at the foot of the sanctuary. She walks, half-stumbling, toward the open sacristy door.

There's much rustling from the pews as the choir finishes the program of hymns, and after a long pause, starts from the beginning. The church is full now, the congregation singing along with the choir.

Absorbed in the words and melody, she's at first unaware of the new sound, a sound she's never heard in church except at funerals. It's a quiet sobbing sound. It seems to stop, then begins again, but now there are muffled words of protest, small shrieks barely heard. Eugenia looks around at the people behind her, though she knows it's not polite. Some people in the front pews look startled, but she can't see anyone weeping.

She thinks perhaps she's imagined the voice. But she hears the sounds again, and a man's voice speaking softly.

The sounds from the sacristy stop for a moment. Eugenia sings
the words of the hymn with a strong voice, though she doesn't
understand all the archaic words, this older, unfamiliar form of
Ukrainian. She's never asked anyone what the words mean.

There! She hears the small voice protesting again. And then
two shrieks. From the pew behind her, where Angela's parents
stand, Mrs. Duma speaks in a frightened whisper to her husband,
"He can't do it. I'm going to her."

A loud hiss from Mr. Duma, then he whispers back to his wife,
"Stay. It's *allowed*. How else can it be?"

The singing becomes quieter, discordant, almost dying away.
A soft wail, muffled by the wall of the sacristy, seems to rise to the
highest reaches of the dome. Then loud sobs and a childish voice
begging, "No! No!"

The small door opens a little, then is slammed shut. There's
silence, then a click of the latch as the priest emerges into the
sanctuary, crying out to the choir, to the congregation. "Louder.
Sing louder!" He holds the glass doorknob tightly behind him
with a white-knuckled hand. He clutches the doorknob with both
hands as someone jerks at it from the other side, trying to open
the door. His surplice is disarranged, a bit of the lace hem caught
up in his trousers. His hair has fallen over his forehead, a swatch
of oily grey. He slides back into the sacristy and the choir sings
loudly, still a little out of tune. There's a rustling from the
congregation behind Eugenia, a shifting of feet. Some of the
men's eyes have a knowing gleam in them. The women study their
prayer books as though seeing them for the first time. Eugenia
thinks she hears Angela sobbing.

The shrieking begins again. It sounds angry now, unrestrained.
There's a sound of wood colliding with wood, of something
falling. Eugenia wonders why Angela is shrieking. The congregation sings. She wants this all to pass, for this strange incident

to become a dream, wants Angela to appear behind her, near her parents, wants this never to have happened.

The sounds from behind the closed door stop. The priest emerges from the sacristy, his vestments tidy. Smoothing his hair. He takes the censor, parades around the altar, sanctifying it with the scented smoke. The Mass begins.

Eugenia tries to sing the responses to the Mass but there's something in her chest, hurting, like vomit about to erupt. Why was Angela crying? The words repeat themselves in the back of her consciousness as prickles of sweat dampen her Sunday clothes.

The Mass goes on for nearly half an hour before the door of the sacristy opens again and Angela emerges. Behind her, she can hear Angela's mother weeping. Angela walks quickly down one of the side aisles to the door of the church. Her face is red and swollen, her expression blank. Her eyes focus on the glossy floor-boards as she hurries out. Softly, the double doors close behind her. Mrs. Duma, ignoring her husband's hissed commands, leaves the pew with a click of sharp heels and walks swiftly down the main aisle, following her daughter.

Theodore and his parents show no sign of having noticed anything unusual. They stare straight ahead, toward the icon of the Virgin, their faces wooden. The Mass continues, but Angela doesn't come back for the sacrament of Communion, nor does her mother return. Eugenia sings only some of the responses. Her mind can no longer feel the presence of angels. It asks her over and over — *Why was Angela crying?*

She's the first one out of the church gate after the Mass, walking home quickly with the sickness lingering deep inside her chest. The light around her is lurid. Its glare gives her pain. Why was Angela crying? She asks herself again and again. *Why was Angela crying?*